D0409516

The Lost Library Book

story by Amanda Bell

illustrations by
Alice Durand-Wietzel

BAINTE DEN STOC
WITHDRAWN FROM
DÚN LAOGHAIRE-RATHDOWN COUNTY
LIBRARY STOCK

Published in Oxford by The Onslaught Press
11 Ridley Road, OX4 2QJ
2017

Text of *The Lost Library Book*, including end matter, © 2017 Amanda Bell

Text of preface © 2017 Jason McElligott

Illustrations © 2017 Alice Durand-Wietzel

This edition © 2017 Mathew Staunton

Amanda Bell (writer) & Alice Durand-Wietzel (illustrator)
assert their moral right to be identified as the authors of this book
in accordance with Section 77 of the Copyright, Designs and Patents Act, 1988.

All rights reserved. No part of this publication may be reproduced, stored
in a retrieval system, or transmitted, in any form or by any means,
electronic, mechanical, photocopying, recording, or
otherwise, without the prior permission in writing of The Onslaught Press,
or as expressly permitted by law, or under terms agreed with the
appropriate reprographics rights organization

ISBN: 978-1-912111-69-5

Typeset in Dr John Fell's **'English' roman** & *italic* types
The roman was cut by Christoffel van Dijck, the italic by Robert Granjon
Both were acquired by Fell in 1672 for the Oxford University Press
The Fell Types are digitally reproduced by Igino Marini. www.iginomarini.com

Designed by Mathew Staunton

Printed and bound by Lightning Source

To the Finder;
and to my mother,
who found treasures for me
in our local library every week.
AB

Surprising Discoveries

If you're not paying attention, it is very easy to walk past the entrance to Marsh's Library, a narrow metal gate in the high stone wall which surrounds the building. This place of quiet in the middle of the busy city of Dublin is crammed full of rare and ancient books.

Marsh's has remained unchanged since it first opened more than 300 years ago, and that is one of the reasons why people come from all over the world to read here. Some of our visitors have been famous, but most have been ordinary people who, like you, happen to love extraordinary books.

The book you are holding in your hands tells the true story of a man who walked in to Marsh's on a bright but cold day in 2012. Under his right arm (I remember it very clearly!) he carried something wrapped up in an old newspaper. "I found this in a junk shop. I think it might belong here," he said. And it did. A very, very old book had come back home after a long absence from its proper place on the shelf.

We have never loaned books. Everything is supposed to stay on the premises, but despite the watchfulness of generations of staff, a small number of books have gone missing.

All of our books have a circular library stamp like the one below. May I ask a favour of you? Will you keep your eyes peeled for anything that should be within the walls of Marsh's? Our missing books are definitely out there somewhere, and they may be hiding in the most unusual of places. You'll get such a warm welcome if you walk in with one of the missing treasures under your arm.

Jason McElligott
The Keeper
Marsh's Library, Dublin

The Lost Library Book

Did you ever forget to return your library books for a week or two? Imagine if you forgot to return your library book *for a hundred years*.

That is exactly what happened to the book in this story.

Way back at the beginning of the 1900s,
a scholar borrowed a book.

He was trying to read a lot of books at the same time, and the books piled up on top of one another beside the desk in his bedroom.

The pile got higher and higher, and the books got dustier and dustier, until one day the pile toppled over with a great crash, and one of the books slid right in underneath his rickety old bed.

The scholar didn't even notice. He was very busy. He never thought about the book again in his whole life, even though he lived to a great old age.

Years after the scholar died, his family decided to sell the house where he had lived. A removal company came in a big lorry to pack up all the furniture.

Piece by piece they packed up tables and chairs, wardrobes and beds, and paintings and flowerpots.

Junk

At last, all that was left were things that had rolled under the furniture years and years ago, and been forgotten about among the dust-balls. Things like odd socks, a few cups and saucers, and some dusty old books. The removal men piled all the bits and pieces into a box, and brought them to a junkshop.

Close to the junkshop lived a man who loved junk. He dropped in nearly every day to see what new treasures had arrived. There was only one thing in the world he loved more than junk, and that was books.

CAT BITES

One lunchtime, the man saw a very old book in the junkshop. It had a brown leather cover with some little holes in it, as if tiny worms had tried to eat it and given up.

In the middle of the front cover was a diamond pattern, and around the edges of the diamond were two rows of little pictures. Hidden among the pictures were the numbers 1537.

1537

Lots of people looked at the book in the junkshop, but no-one could figure out what it was about. It was written in a strange alphabet. The man was very curious. He visited the shop every day that week to look at the book.

On the Friday he decided to buy it.

“I don’t know what you’re going to do with that,” said the shop-keeper, “what use is it if you can’t understand it?”

When he got the book home he wiped off the layer of dust with a soft cloth. Then he set it down on a table and carefully opened the leather cover.

The pages were heavy to turn. He didn't recognize the writing. In fact the only thing that he could understand was a big capital letter at the beginning of each chapter. Around the letters were leaves, and strange little creatures with human heads and animal hooves. There were a lot of scribbles in the margins, and scraps of paper had been attached to the pages with little pieces of wire.

On the first page was a picture of two dragons holding a shield. The dragons had feathers on their necks, long curly tails, and heads like cockerels. They were standing beneath a tree. Beside the picture of the dragons was a circle, and in the circle were the words 'MARSH'S LIBRARY'. The man decided to call in to Marsh's Library the next day to find out more.

The library was hard to find. The man walked along past St Patrick's Cathedral until he came to a large granite archway. Hidden in the archway was a cast iron gate.

He pushed the gate open with a creak.

He climbed up the steps and walked through a garden full of flowering trees before, at long last, he reached the door to the library. It was like stepping into another time.

The air smelt of pepper. Tall ladders leaned against dark wooden bookcases which stretched up towards the ceiling. A long aisle led through the middle of the bookcases. The man walked along the aisle, looking around him with wide eyes. The only sound was the ticking of a clock. He passed by enormous books with brass hinges, and glass-topped cabinets full of strange instruments.

Out of the corner of his eye he glimpsed a knobbly white object. When he looked closer, he saw that it was a human skull. He walked a little faster.

At the very end of the long room he found the librarian. “Hello,” he said, nervously, “I have something you might be interested in.” He took the newspaper-wrapped package out of his rucksack.

When the librarian opened the parcel, his eyes lit up like stars.

The librarian came out from behind his desk, took the man by the elbow and brought him over to a bookshelf. On the bookshelf were four books that looked exactly like the book from the junkshop.

XII

I
II
III
V

"There should be five," he said. "The fifth book disappeared over a hundred years ago, and now you have found it."

"Nearly four hundred years ago," the librarian continued, "these books were owned by a doctor called Theodore Gulston. He was a very serious doctor, and he wanted to learn everything there was to know about medicine. He was studying these books because they were the most famous medical books in the world for over a thousand years. As he studied the books, he made notes, and to keep his notes safe he attached them to the pages of his books with little pins. This makes them very important books indeed. Now that you have found the missing book, people from all over the world will want to come and see it. That is, of course, if you will let us keep it."

The man really loved books. He loved reading them, and he loved collecting them. He loved the writing, and he loved the pictures. He loved the smell of them, and he loved the feel of them. But this was the only book of its kind in the whole world, and lots of other people would want to see it too.

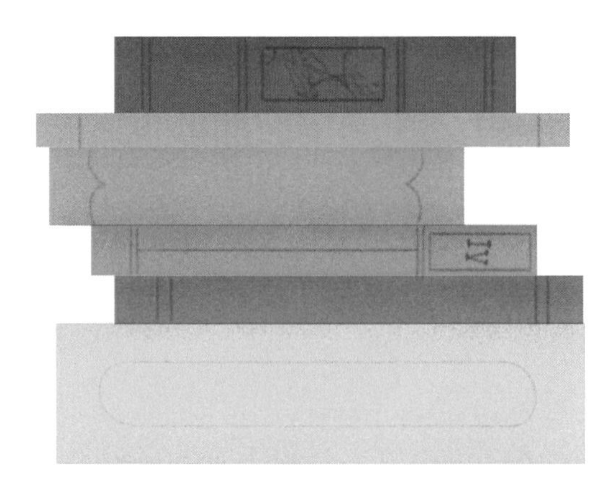

He looked at the book, and he looked at the librarian. "Of course," he said, "I would be delighted." And he was. He still calls in to the junkshop every day on his way home, and he can visit the book in Marsh's Library whenever he wants to.

And so can you.

Further Information

The missing book was one of the volumes of *Galeni Librorum*, a medical encyclopedia written by a philosopher and physician known as Galen of Pergamum. He was born in Anatolia (which is now in Turkey) in around 129AD and died around 200AD. His first job was as a surgeon to the gladiators. He later became the personal physician of the Roman emperor Marcus Aurelius. He studied all of the Greek and Roman medical texts available at the time, and wrote about eighty medical books himself, many of which have been lost. His books were written by hand. They were the most important medical textbooks in existence for over a thousand years, and were finally printed, in Greek, for the first time in the 1500s.

Theodore Gulston (1572-1632) was an English scholar and physician. He set out to study and improve the works of Galen. The five volumes of Galen's works that Gulston was working on were published in Basle in Switzerland in 1537. They are written in Greek. Gulston wrote his notes in Greek too, in the margins of the books, and also on separate sheets of paper, which he pinned to the pages. In 1635, his widow Helena donated the books to Merton College, Oxford. Some years later, they became the property of Archbishop Narcissus Marsh, who put them in his library in Dublin.

Marsh's Library opened in 1707 and was the first public library in Ireland. The library contains over 25,000 books from the 1500s, 1600s and 1700s. A lot of the books are about medicine, law, science, travel, maths, and music.

You can find a full list of the books in Marsh's Library on their website,

www.marshlibrary.ie/catalogue

Marsh's was never a lending library–you can only read the books when you are in the building. The books are so precious that sometimes students were locked into 'cages' to read them. In 1863 a man called George Mathews was sentenced to a year of hard labour in prison for taking a book out of the library without permission. The missing library book in this story should never have been removed from the building–perhaps it was lent as a special favour.

Today, Marsh's Library welcomes visitors of all ages.

Acknowledgements

Huge thanks to Mathew Staunton for taking on the story and matching it with Alice's charming illustrations, to Jason McElligott for his support, Síne Quinn for her editorial expertise, and to readers Clare Bell, Elizabeth Gageby Bell, Lia O'Hegarty, and Jonathan Ryder. Thanks also to Brian Kirk, Ger Nichol, Faith O'Grady, Kieran Owens, Robert Towers and Sarah Webb for their advice–their expertise is much appreciated.

AB, January 2017

Lightning Source UK Ltd.
Milton Keynes UK
UKRC01n0137220817
307704UK00002B/3